Bill Martin Jr, Ph.D., has devoted his life to the education of young children. *Bill Martin Books* reflect his philosophy: that children's imaginations are opened up through the play of language, the imagery of illustration, and the permanent joy of reading books.

Text copyright © 1988 by Eve Merriam / Illustrations copyright © 1992 by Dale Gottlieb
All rights reserved, including the right to reproduce this book or portions thereof in any form.
The poem "Train Leaves the Station" was previously published in 1988 by William Morrow and Co., Inc., in a collection entitled *You Be Good & I'll Be Night.*
Published by Henry Holt and Company, Inc., 115 West 18th Street, New York, New York 10011.
Published simultaneously in Canada by Fitzhenry & Whiteside Ltd.,
91 Granton Drive, Richmond Hill, Ontario L4B 2N5.

Library of Congress Cataloging-in-Publication Data
Merriam, Eve.   Train leaves the station / by Eve Merriam; illustrated by Dale Gottlieb.   "A Bill Martin book"
    Summary: A toy train and its occupants make a journey that introduces the numbers one to ten.
    ISBN 0-8050-1934-0   [1. Railroads—Trains—Fiction.   2. Toys—Fiction.   3. Counting.   4. Stories in rhyme.]
I. Gottlieb, Dale, ill.   II. Title.   PZ8.3. M55187Tr 1992   [E]—dc20   91-28009

Printed in the United States of America on acid-free paper.∞
First Edition   10 9 8 7 6 5 4 3 2 1

EVE MERRIAM

TRAIN
LEAVES THE
STATION

Illustrated by
DALE GOTTLIEB

1

Hunter on the horse, fox on the run,

train leaves the station at one-o-one.

2 Buckle on the belt, lace in the shoe,

train leaves the station at two-o-two.

3 Worm in the garden, apple on the tree,

train leaves the station at three-o-three.

4 Light on the ceiling, rug on the floor,

train leaves the station at four-o-four.

5

Berry on the bush, honey in the hive,

train leaves the station at five-o-five.

6 Salt in the ocean, clay in the bricks,

train leaves the station at six-o-six.

7

Snake in the grass, angel in heaven,

train leaves the station
at seven-o-seven.

Ink in the pen, chalk on the slate,

train leaves the station at eight-o-eight.

9

Sand in the desert, coal in the mine,

train leaves the station at nine-o-nine.

Cow in the barn, bear in the den,

train got stuck at the station again.

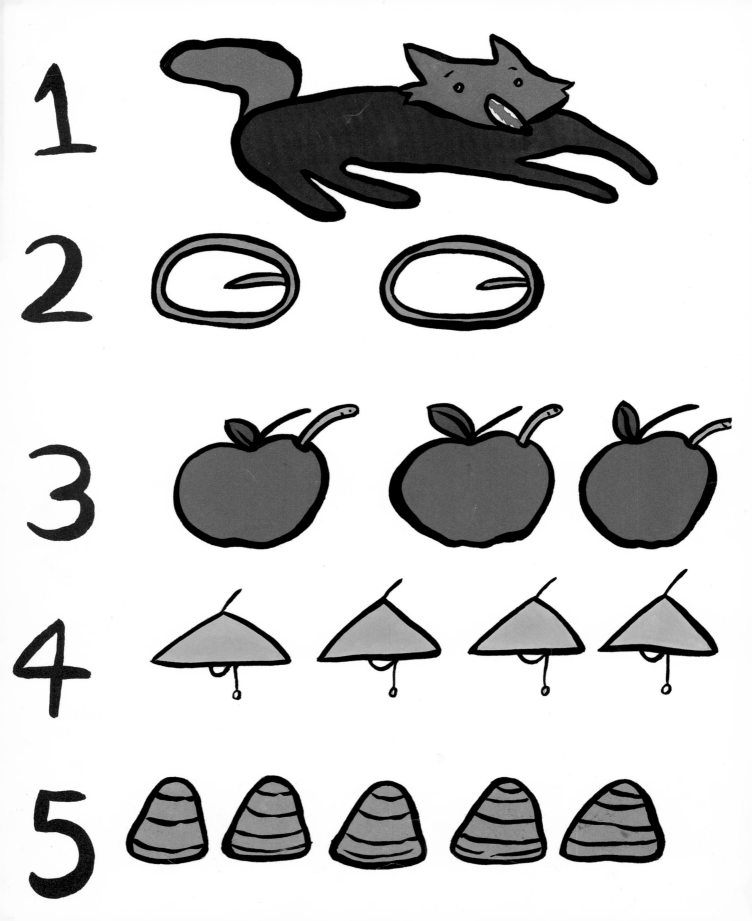

6
7
8
9
10